Pink is for Boys

by Willa Liburd Tavernier

Illustrated by Audeva Joseph

Published by Willa Liburd Tavernier
Bloomington, Indiana
willa@nattakm.com

First Edition

ISBN
978-976-96597-0-4

LOC Control Number
2021901584

Dedication

To my sons, who surprise me every day.

Acknowledgments

I am so grateful to Nathan and Julie Machart for their friendship, and for reading and revising this manuscript.

Much love to my St. Kitts posse, especially Jeweleen who always shares her kids with mine on visits home, and who's been prodding me to publish for over a decade.

And especially for the contributions of my husband H. Vincent Tavernier whose ideas greatly enriched the final version of this book.

Jamilla and Jeremy are good friends. So are their moms. Jamilla lives in St. Kitts. Jeremy lives in Tortola.

Jeremy comes to St. Kitts on the plane.

Jeremy and Jamilla love to play together.

Jeremy and Jamilla are in the back of Jamilla's mommy's car. Their mommies are in the front.

Jamilla has a pink puppy, with a computer inside. It is her favourite toy this week.

Jeremy wants a turn with the puppy. Jamilla says, "No. It's not for boys. It's pink".

"But pink is my favourite colour!" says Jeremy. "Pink is for girls," says Jamilla. "Blue is for boys".

Jeremy asks his mommy "is it true, Mommy?" "No-o-o" their mommies both say. "Boys and girls can like any colour".

They have reached to Jeremy's grandma's house. "See you tomorrow, Jeremy" says Jamilla.

"Hmph!" says Jeremy. He is mad because he did not get to play with the pink puppy.

The next day Jeremy and his mommy go to Jamilla's house. Jamilla has just come home from dance class. "I go to dance class too, in Tortola," Jeremy says.

"Noooooo." says Jamilla "You go to karate class. Only girls have dance class. Boys go to karate class."

Jeremy says "No! I go to dance class."
"Mo-o-o-o-mmy!" Jamilla shouts.

"I told Jeremy he goes to karate class, but he keeps saying he goes to dance class, and boys can't go to dance class. They go to karate class!"

Jamilla's mommy laughs. "Oh boy! We need both of you to calm down. Can you do that?" Jeremy and Jamilla nod.

Then Jamilla's mom says "Lots of boys dance, Jamilla. If boys don't dance, who will the girls dance with?"

Jeremy's mommy says "Jeremy does go to dance class Jamilla. And you know what there are lots of boys and only one girl in that class. They do lots of fun dances, and they learn all the latest hip-hop moves!"

Jamilla has changed out of her dance clothes. She is going to play with Jeremy. She brings her pink puppy for Jeremy to have a turn.

Jeremy loves the learning games on the puppy's computer. Jamilla plays with a doll.

Jeremy is tired of playing with the puppy.

"May I have another toy?" he asks.

"Do you want my doll?" Jamilla holds it out to Jeremy.

"No!" Jeremy exclaims, "dolls are for girls. Don't you have any trucks?"

IN THE PLAYROOM WITH
JAMILLA & JEREMY

In '*Pink is for Boys*' Jamilla and Jeremy have a conflict over the things boys and girls can do or play with. Their mommies help them to calm down, and to make a better choice about their behaviour.

Maybe you have a big brother or sister, aunt, uncle, grandmother, friend or mommy or daddy who helps you at home!

GLOSSARY

CONFLICT a strong disagreement.
Jeremy gets very upset when Jamilla says that dance class is only for girls, and karate class is only for boys. Jeremy has a strong disagreement with Jamilla because of this.

CHOICE the act of picking between two or more possibilities.
Jamilla listens to her mommy and Jeremy's mommy. She makes a choice to change the way she thinks about what boys can do. She shares her toy with Jeremy even though it is pink.

CALM not excited, peaceful.
After Jeremy and Jamilla calm down they can listen to their mommies and to each other. They have more fun playing together when they calm down.

MORE TO THINK ABOUT

Jeremy is upset when Jamilla says he can't play with a pink toy or go to dance class because he is a boy. But in the end he refuses to play with a doll and says that dolls are for girls!

What do you think about that?

How would you feel if you were Jamilla?

Has anyone ever told you that you should not do something because you are not a boy or because you are not a girl? How did that make you feel?

If that has never happened to you how would you feel if it did?

Sometimes drawing a picture about your feelings can help. If you would like to, you can use the next page to draw.

QUICK FACTS ABOUT
ST. KITTS AND NEVIS
&
THE BRITISH VIRGIN ISLANDS

In 'Pink is for Boys' Jeremy and his mommy travel from Tortola to St. Kitts. Have you ever traveled away from home before? In a car? On a plane? On a boat?

St. Kitts is an island that is part of St. Kitts and Nevis. Tortola is an island that is part of the Virgin Islands, which is an Overseas Territory of the United Kingdom, also called the British Virgin Islands. An island is surrounded by water. The British Virgin Islands and St. Kitts and Nevis are surrounded by the Caribbean Sea.

The Caribbean Sea is a sea bordered by Central America, the West Indies and South America. The islands in the Caribbean Sea are called the West Indies.

To get from St. Kitts and Nevis to the British Virgin Islands people travel on a plane or by boat.

Would you like to travel to the Caribbean someday? What would you bring with you?

I would like to travel to

I would bring

Look at the map on the next page to see the
many West Indian islands you can visit.

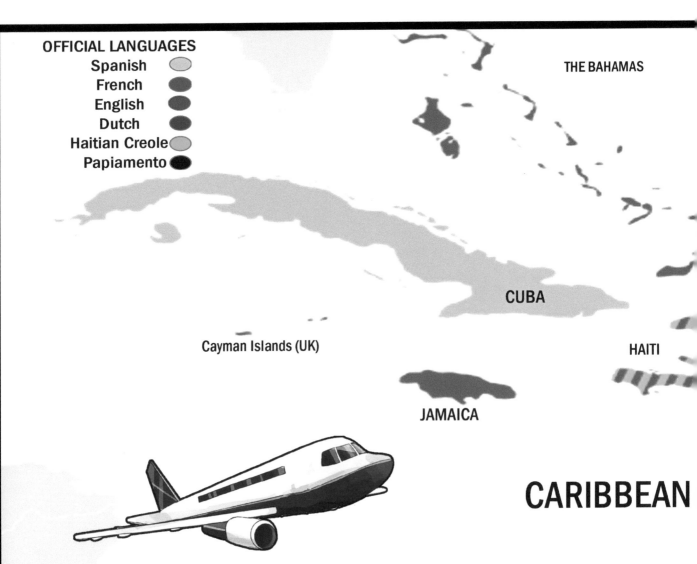

OFFICIAL LANGUAGES

Spanish
French
English
Dutch
Haitian Creole
Papiamento

THE BAHAMAS

CUBA

Cayman Islands (UK)

HAITI

JAMAICA

CARIBBEAN

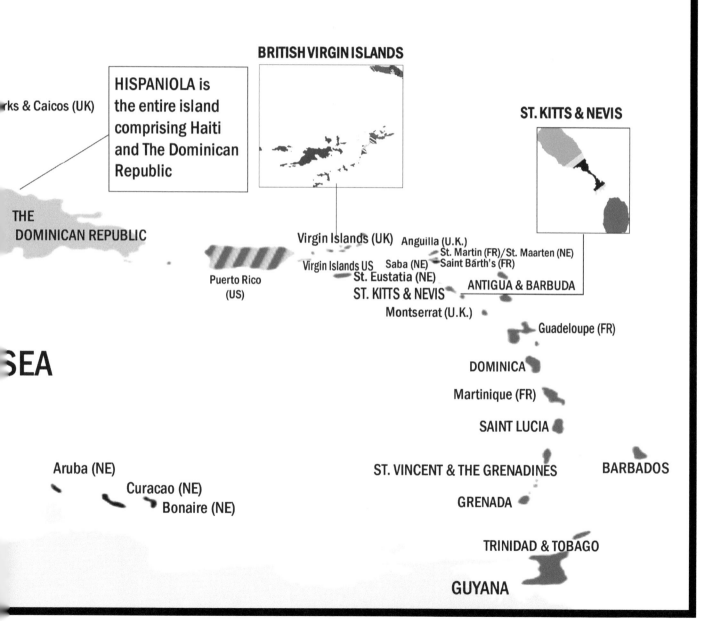

MAP OF THE WEST INDIES
with inset flag maps of the British Virgin Islands and St. Kitts and Nevis

BRITISH VIRGIN ISLANDS

rks & Caicos (UK)

HISPANIOLA is the entire island comprising Haiti and The Dominican Republic

ST. KITTS & NEVIS

THE DOMINICAN REPUBLIC

Virgin Islands (UK)   Anguilla (U.K.)
St. Martin (FR)/St. Maarten (NE)
Virgin Islands US   Saba (NE)   Saint Bárth's (FR)
Puerto Rico   St. Eustatia (NE)
(US)   **ST. KITTS & NEVIS**   **ANTIGUA & BARBUDA**

Montserrat (U.K.)

SEA

Guadeloupe (FR)

DOMINICA

Martinique (FR)

SAINT LUCIA

Aruba (NE)

ST. VINCENT & THE GRENADINES   **BARBADOS**

Curacao (NE)
Bonaire (NE)   **GRENADA**

TRINIDAD & TOBAGO

GUYANA

PAINT OR COLOUR

THE END

CPSIA information can be obtained
at www.ICGtesting.com
Printed in the USA
BVHW021322081221
623552BV00002B/32